I0824490
Like a Pro
Archery
Jessica Coupé
AV2
www.openlightbox.com

Step 1
Go to **www.openlightbox.com**

Step 2
Enter this unique code
NOYMFWDBX

Step 3
Explore your interactive eBook!

AV2
Like a Pro
Archery
Start!
Share

AV2 is optimized for use on any device

Your interactive eBook comes with...

Audio
Listen to the entire book read aloud

Videos
Watch informative video clips

Weblinks
Gain additional information for research

Try This!
Complete activities and hands-on experiments

Key Words
Study vocabulary, and complete a matching word activity

Quizzes
Test your knowledge

Slideshows
View images and captions

Share
Share titles within your Learning Management System (LMS) or Library Circulation System

Citation
Create bibliographical references following APA, CMOS, and MLA styles

This title is part of our AV2 digital subscription

1-Year K–5 Subscription
ISBN 978-1-7911-3320-7

Access hundreds of AV2 titles with our digital subscription.
Sign up for a FREE trial at **www.openlightbox.com/trial**

The digital components of this book are guaranteed to stay active for at least five years from the date of publication.

Contents

I love archery.
I am going to do archery today.

Archery has been around for more than 20,000 years.

I get dressed for archery practice. I wear a top and pants.

Archery ranges have dress codes. These help keep archers safe.

I have a bow and arrows. I keep the arrows in a bag called a quiver.

An archer may wear a thumb ring or arm guard for protection.

I practice archery at the archery range. I shoot arrows at targets.

Pro archers shoot at targets up to 295 feet (90 meters) away.

I warm up before starting to shoot. I stretch to loosen my muscles.

Pro archers practice several days each week.

I place the notched end of the arrow on the string and pull it back. Then, I let the string go. The arrow flies toward the target.

At events, pro archers take turns shooting their arrows.

I shoot an arrow at the target. I score points if I hit near the center.

In events, the archer with the most points after everyone has shot all their arrows wins.

Sometimes, I shoot on a team with friends.

Teammates add their points together after they shoot.

I love archery.

ARCHERY FACTS

These pages provide more detail about interesting facts found in the book. They are intended to be used by adults as a learning support to help young readers round out their knowledge of each sport featured in the *Like a Pro* series.

Pages 4–5

Getting Ready Archery is a sport in which a person shoots an arrow from a bow at a target that is a set distance away. Bows and arrows have been used to hunt animals for thousands of years. Today, archery is also a sport. There are several types of archery. In target archery, archers shoot at a non-moving target.

Pages 6–7

What I Wear Most archery ranges have a dress code. Archers need to wear clothing that will not get in the way of their bow string. They should not wear baggy clothing, and long hair must be tied back. Archers may wear short or long-sleeved tops with shorts or pants. Archers are not allowed to wear flip-flops or other open-toed shoes.

Pages 8–9

What I Use An archer needs a bow, arrows, and a quiver. A quiver is often carried on the back. Bows vary in height, according to the type of bow and the length of the archer's draw. A draw is how far an archer pulls back the bowstring before releasing. The size of the arrows depend on the size and strength of the bow.

Pages 10–11

At the Range Archery events are held at archery ranges. These may be indoors or outdoors, and include targets for archers to shoot at. Whistles are used to instruct archers at some ranges. Two short whistles mean archers can get ready, while one short whistle means "begin shooting." Three short whistles mean archers can retrieve their arrows. Four short whistles mean an emergency has occurred.

Pages 12–13

Warming Up Archery uses a large amount of upper body strength. It is important to warm up before playing. Warming up helps oxygen reach the player's muscles, loosening them. This reduces the chance of injury. Tight muscles may also affect an archer's ability to hit a target. Archers should also stretch their upper back, shoulders, and arms.

Pages 14–15

Shooting an Arrow In indoor target archery, archers shoot between 30 and 60 arrows at a target. These are shot over several rounds, with three to six arrows in each. The target is between 5.5 and 27 feet (18 and 90 meters) away from the archer. Targets are divided into 10 zones. Players score points depending where their arrow lands on the target.

Pages 16–17

On Target At the end of the game, archers add their scores from each round. The inner circle is worth 10 points, while the outer circle is worth 1. The archer who gets the most points wins. There are usually three archers assigned to a target. One, the captain, calls the score. The other two record the scores the captain calls out. Sometimes, a fourth player, the observer, makes sure the arrows are called and scored correctly.

Pages 18–19

Team Games Archery is sometimes played as a team sport. Usually, three people form a team. Teams may be all male, all female, or mixed. Team members take turns shooting two arrows each at the target. Often, a team has only two minutes to shoot all their arrows. After all rounds have finished, the team with the most total points wins.

Pages 20–21

I Love Archery Archery helps players stay active and healthy. Playing archery strengthens hand, arm, and upper back muscles. It also promotes hand-eye coordination and helps players learn to focus. As archers practice, they learn patience. In order to get the most from archery, it is important for players to eat healthy foods, such as fruits and vegetables, to help them perform at their best.

KEY WORDS

Research has shown that as much as 65 percent of all written material published in English is made up of 300 words. These 300 words cannot be taught using pictures or learned by sounding them out. They must be recognized by sight. This book contains 55 common sight words to help young readers improve their reading fluency and comprehension. This book also teaches young readers several important content words, such as proper nouns. These words are paired with pictures to aid in learning and improve understanding.

Page	Sight Words First Appearance
4	am, do, I, to
5	a, around, been, for, has, like, more, than, years
6	and, get
7	have, help, keep, these
8	in, the
9	an, may, or
10	at
11	away, feet, up
12	before, my
13	days, each
14	back, end, go, it, let, of, on, place, then
15	take, their, turns
16	if, near, points
17	after, all, most, with
18	sometimes
17	add, they, together

Page	Content Words First Appearance
4	archery
6	pants, practice, top
7	archers, archery ranges, dress codes
8	arrows, bag, bow, quiver
9	arm guard, thumb ring
10	targets
12	muscles
13	week
14	string
15	events
16	center
18	friends, team
19	teammates

Published by Lightbox Learning Inc.
276 5th Avenue, Suite 704 #917
New York, NY 10001
Website: www.openlightbox.com

Library of Congress Control Number: 2023935735

ISBN 978-1-7911-5784-5 (hardcover)
ISBN 978-1-7911-5785-2 (softcover)
ISBN 978-1-7911-5786-9 (multi-user eBook)

042023
100922

Printed in Guangzhou, China
1 2 3 4 5 6 7 8 9 0 27 26 25 24 23

Project Coordinator: John Willis
Designer: Ana María Vidal

Every reasonable effort has been made to trace ownership and to obtain permission to reprint copyright material. The publisher would be pleased to have any errors or omissions brought to its attention so that they may be corrected in subsequent printings.

The publisher acknowledges Alamy, Bridgeman Images, Dreamstime, Getty Images, and Shutterstock as its primary image suppliers for this title.